small *world* bug life

INSIGHT KIDS
An Earth Aware Book

San Rafael, California

The brightly colored little beetle launches herself up, up, and away. She skims over a farmer's full fields on her tiny beating wings. Below her, rows of cabbages and leafy lettuces and clusters of tomatoes grow round and ripe in the summer sun.

This little insect is a ladybug. She is hungry, but not for the farmer's food. A broad green leaf is her landing pad, and juicy bugs are her prey.

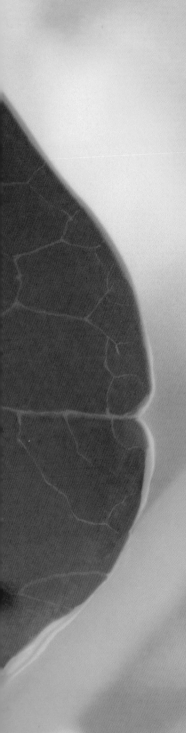

The little ladybug lowers her six-legged landing gear. She touches down lightly on a swaying green leaf. The jagged claws on her spindly legs get a good grip.

With a click-clack, the ladybug's delicate flying wings fold away beneath her spotted armor. There are seven black polka dots on the fiery-red wing cases of this little ladybug. These hard front wings shield her soft body and her see-through flying wings.

The little ladybug explores
the tangle of leafy plants around
her. She crawls across long leaves
that arch and bend like living bridges.
She climbs spear-shaped leaves that
shoot straight and tall into the sky.

Then the little ladybug lifts and swivels
her fiery-red front wings, ready for takeoff.
Beneath them, her paper-thin back wings unfold
and flutter like a fan until she rises into the air.

The tiny ladybug beats her transparent wings up to 85 times per second as she flies.

The little ladybug lands softly
on a delicate strawberry flower.
She will crawl inside and walk
across the bed of sticky pollen
at the center of the flower.

She usually hunts bugs for her breakfast, but today she can feed on sweet nectar and tiny grains of pollen. The sticky pollen clings to the hairs on her legs. It will rub off on the next strawberry flower she visits, and soon brand-new strawberries will grow.

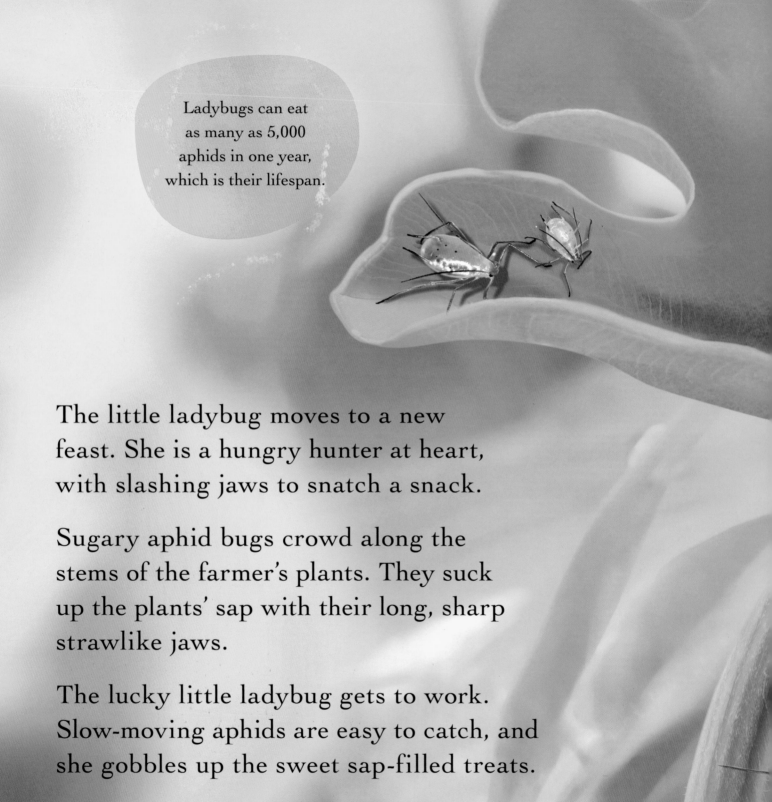

Ladybugs can eat as many as 5,000 aphids in one year, which is their lifespan.

The little ladybug moves to a new feast. She is a hungry hunter at heart, with slashing jaws to snatch a snack.

Sugary aphid bugs crowd along the stems of the farmer's plants. They suck up the plants' sap with their long, sharp strawlike jaws.

The lucky little ladybug gets to work. Slow-moving aphids are easy to catch, and she gobbles up the sweet sap-filled treats.

The little ladybug must look out for danger though! Even tiny aphids have a way to eat and not be eaten. Busy ants are their bodyguards, and sweet honeydew is their trade.

The sap-sucking aphids release glistening droplets of honeydew that the ants like to eat. In return, the ants work like shepherds to keep their herd of aphids safe from attack. They can flip and tip a not-so-lucky ladybug off her feet and away from her prey.

It is not unusual for a female ladybug to lay as many as 2,000 eggs in her lifetime.

The little ladybug crawls into the shade of an umbrella-like leaf. It is cool and safe beneath the wide, green leaf, and she has a special job to do.

The underside of the leaf is a perfect hiding place to lay a cluster of tiny cream-colored eggs. And the plant, where many aphids live, is the perfect pantry for her hungry hatchlings.

The little ladybug's eggs turn from cream to deep golden yellow as the babies, called larvae, grow inside them. But do fiery-red seven-spotted ladybugs fly out from those eggs? No!

The ladybug's babies look like fierce little crocodiles when they hatch. They are creepy and crawly. They are bumpy and bristly. They scurry about hunting for food, and their jaws are ready to munch.

The hungry little grubs eat and grow until each one is squashed inside its firm skin. They squeeze out of that skin and grow a new, bigger skin. Before long they are too big for that skin as well and so they must squeeze out again. Then the fat larva finally finds a magical changing place in the shadows beneath a leaf. There it changes into a pupa.

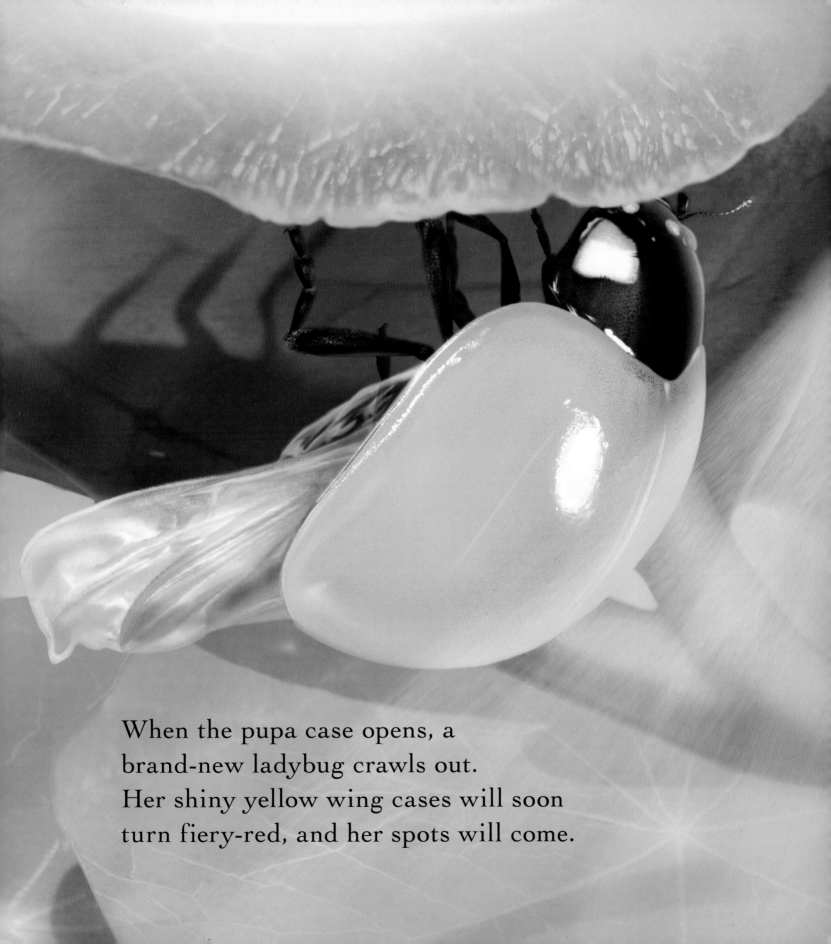

When the pupa case opens, a
brand-new ladybug crawls out.
Her shiny yellow wing cases will soon
turn fiery-red, and her spots will come.

The brand-new ladybug has seven black spots now. She stretches out her bright wings and whirls over the farmer's fields. She explores the swishing leaves of her growing green home.

But suddenly heavy raindrops fall from a a stormy sky, and the brave little beetle looks for shelter. She joins a cluster of ladybugs huddling beneath the curve of an arching leaf. They are safe from the wind and rain there.

Ladybugs are in danger of being hunted by birds – but frogs, wasps, and spiders hunt them, too.

But the big wide sky holds other dangers for a little ladybug. Even though the bold colors of her fiery-red wings flash out a warning, a hungry bird swoops. "Don't dare to eat me!" the brightly colored little insect says.

Ladybugs taste bad. They ooze out a foul-smelling fluid from their body when predators come close. If they are really frightened, ladybugs stop, drop, and roll into a hiding place where they play dead.

Other dangers lie, like sticky, tricky traps among the lush green plants. The birds, beetles, and bugs are hungry, but the spinning spiders are hungry, too.

The see-through strands of a silky web are slung between two stems, and a watching orb-web spider waits. There is little chance of escape for an unlucky ladybug that flies into the sticky threads of this wide web.

The storm has passed, and the flowers unfurl their golden petals in the sun's warm rays. The little ladybug climbs up a gently swaying stalk, looking for a supply of tasty bugs to eat.

Other kinds of ladybugs share her leafy hunting ground. Most prey on bugs, but some nibble on the farmer's plants. Colorful wing cases protect the smooth dome-shaped bodies of these ladybugs, too. Some are spotted and others are striped.

The fiery-red ladybugs have helped keep the farmer's crops healthy and pest-free. It is a good harvest for the farmer, and his little spotted friends have eaten well, too.

As the days grow colder and autumn leaves float gently to the ground, thousands of little ladybugs gather in the cracks and crevices of trees. They crawl beneath loose bark and snuggle under blankets of dry leaves. They feel safe and warm huddled together.

The hungry little ladybugs wake with the first burst of spring. They have slept through the dark cold days of winter, and now the scent of a new season is in the air.

There are young green plants to explore, and the nectar of spring's first flowers to sip.

The little ladybug lifts and swivels her fiery-red wings. Her delicate flying wings unfold and she takes off once more over the farmer's fresh fields.

INSIGHT KIDS
An Earth Aware Book

PO Box 3088
San Rafael, CA 94912
www.insighteditions.com

www.MANDALAEARTHEDITIONS.com
FOR WEB EXCLUSIVE CONTENT!

www.facebook.com/InsightEditions
@insighteditions

First published in the United States in 2013 by Insight Editions
Copyright © 2012 Weldon Owen Pty Ltd
Originally published in Great Britain in 2012 by Weldon Owen Pty Ltd

Text by Lynette Evans
Illustrations by Francesca D'Ottavi/Wilkinson Studios

Library of Congress Cataloging-in-Publication Data available.

ISBN: 978-1-60887-199-5

ROOTS of PEACE   REPLANTED PAPER

Insight Editions, in association with Roots of Peace, will plant two
trees for each tree used in the manufacturing of this book. Roots of
Peace is an internationally renowned humanitarian organization
dedicated to eradicating land mines worldwide and converting
war-torn lands into productive farms and wildlife habitats. Roots of
Peace will plant two million fruit and nut trees in Afghanistan and
provide farmers there with the skills and support necessary for
sustainable land use.

Manufactured in China

10 9 8 7 6 5 4 3 2 1